STERLING CHILDREN'S BOOKS
New York

An Imprint of Sterling Publishing Co., Inc.
1166 Avenue of the Americas
New York, NY 10036

Text © 2018 Laura Sassi
Cover and interior illustrations © 2018 Rebecca Gerlings

ISBN 978-1-4549-2200-1

Distributed in Canada by Sterling Publishing Co., Inc.
$^{c}/o$ Canadian Manda Group, 664 Annette Street
Toronto, Ontario M6S 2C8, Canada
Distributed in the United Kingdom by GMC Distribution Services
Castle Place, 166 High Street, Lewes, East Sussex BN7 1XU, England
Distributed in Australia by NewSouth Books
45 Beach Street, Coogee, NSW 2034, Australia

For information about custom editions, special sales, and premium and
corporate purchases, please contact Sterling Special Sales at 800-805-5489
or specialsales@sterlingpublishing.com.

Manufactured in China
Lot #:
10 9 8 7 6 5 4 3 2 1
12/17

sterlingpublishing.com

Cover and interior design by Heather Kelly

The artwork for this book was created using
airbrush, ink, and Photoshop.

For Jonathan. —L. S.
For Mum and Dad. —R. G.

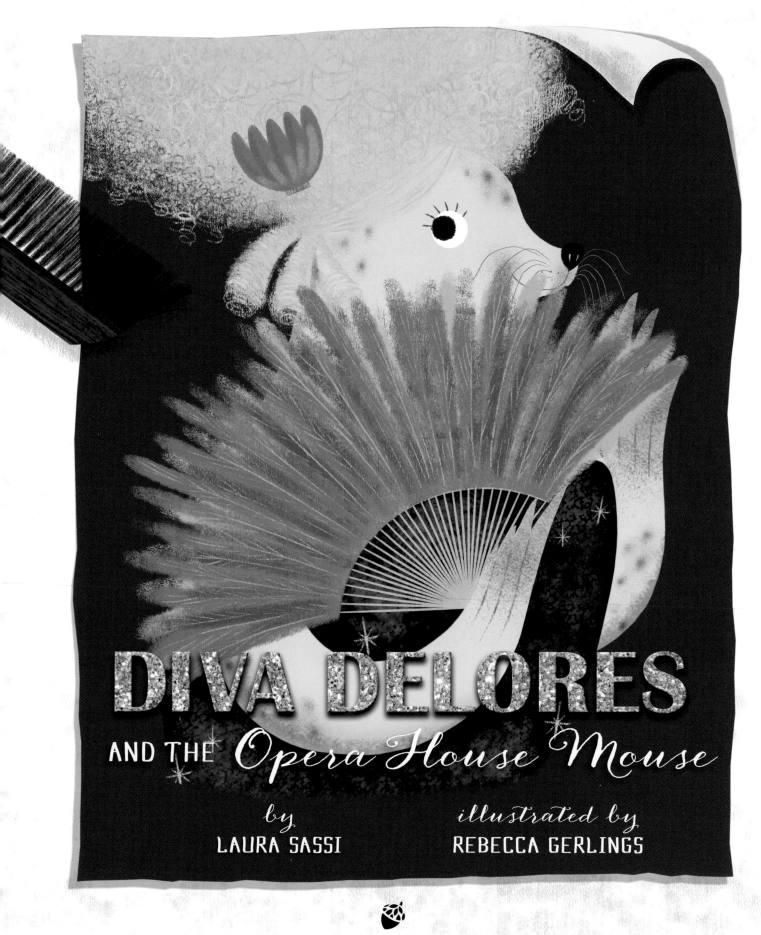

DIVA DELORES
AND THE *Opera House Mouse*

by
LAURA SASSI

illustrated by
REBECCA GERLINGS

STERLING CHILDREN'S BOOKS
New York

Fernando loved chocolate
and cheese on dry toast,
and popcorn and gumdrops,
but what he liked most . . .

was feasting on Mozart,
Puccini, and Strauss,
and lending a paw
at the Old Opera House.

Delores loved glamour and
spotlights and praise.
She longed to be showered
with fragrant bouquets.

Now here was her chance,
after years in the chorus,
to take center stage and be
Diva Delores!

Me-me-me-me!

And yet, when Fernando
said, "How do you do?
I'm here to assist
with your diva debut . . ."

Delores said, "Nonsense!"
and left in a huff.
"A *mouse* help a *diva*?
That's not good enough!"

No-no-no-no!

At practice next morning,
she hit her notes wrong.
She missed her grand entrance
and flubbed her last song.

Fla-fla-fla-FLUB!

The cast was aghast . . .
then from deep in the house
came a squeak, "Let me help!
I'm the Opera House Mouse!"

With a swish of his tail
he wrote out each cue,
and—presto!—Delores
knew just what do.

Tra-la-la-la!

The cast and the maestro
were greatly relieved,
but Diva Delores,
quite frankly, was peeved.

She bellowed and bawled.
"You helped me, it's true,
but a *mouse* help a *diva*?
That simply won't do!"

Now shoo-shoo-shoo-shoo-shoo!

With one day remaining
till opening night,
Delores discovered . . .
her gown was too tight!

Fernando rushed in
with ribbons and lace.
Then like a fine tailor,
he wove in more space.

The gown was perfection.
Delores still fussed.
"I deserve *bigger* help.
Proper size is a must!"

Then grabbing a bottle
of stinky perfume,
she spritzed poor Fernando
right out of the room!

Ta-ta-ta-ta!

Fernando trudged home,
in a terrible mood.
"I'm ready to quit.
That Delores is rude!"

But as he sat moping
alone in his house,
he thought about Mozart,
Puccini, and Strauss.

"If I stop helping now,
the show won't succeed.
I can't give up yet—
there's an opera in need!"

But first . . .

"Delores," he said,
in a voice strong and brave,
"If I'm going to help you,
you have to behave."

"For starters, I'd like to hear
thank you and *please*
when I help fix your dress
or bring crackers and cheese."

Delores was stunned.
Could Fernando be right?
She needed to think,
so she bid him good night.

So lo-lo-lo-long!

Next morning was show day,
and make no mistake,
Delores had jitters.
She felt her legs shake.

She tried sucking candies.
She tried sipping tea.
She looked for Fernando.
Oh, where could he be?

Now standing on stage
as the orchestra played,
Delores felt faint.
First she swooned . . .
then she swayed.

She opened her mouth,
but nothing came out.
Not a word. Not a sound.
Then she spotted . . .

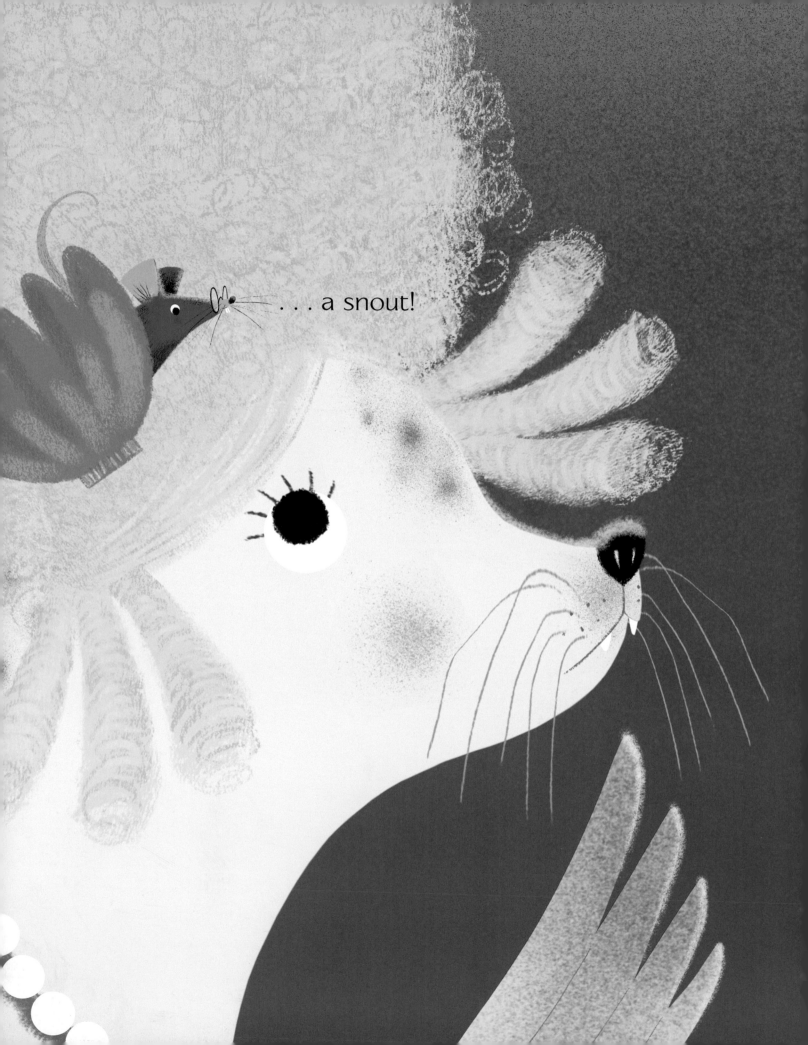

. . . a snout!

From out of her wig followed
ears, paws, and tail.
"You can do it," he squeaked.
Then her singing . . .

set sail!

Voilà-la-la-la!

She sang high, she sang low,
with a voice rich and sweet,
as the Opera House Mouse
tapped along to the beat.

And when she forgot
the last verse of her song,
he said, "I can help!"
Then he *tra-la*'d along.

And the audience loved them.
They brought down the house.
"Three cheers for Delores!"
"Three cheers for that mouse!"

"Now *that*," said Delores,
"was a diva debut.
I couldn't have done it,
dear mouse, without you."

Thank-you-you-you!

Then heaving a sigh
that was humble and true,
she said, "I'm so sorry.
Can we start anew?"

"Of course!" cheered Fernando,
with kindness and ease.
"We'll make a great pair—
just like carrots and peas!"

"Just like pretzels and salt!"
"Just like coffee and cream!"
"We'll be Diva and Mouse . . .

. . . the Opera House team!"